AF438860

Turtleberry Press

Baltimore, MD 21234

www.turtleberrypress.com

Melinda likes to sit and look out her window. She especially likes to watch her cute neighbor come and go. Will she ever get the nerve and opportunity to talk to him?

6:30 am Thursday

He walked out of his house in basketball shorts and a tank top. He had a garment bag, a small duffel bag, and a briefcase with him. I sat back in my chair and propped my feet up as he walked to his car. My view was perfect. I got to admire how great his legs looked. He had thick muscular thighs and calves that looked like he was a runner. His back looked like he lifted weights. Watching his muscles flex while he put his things in his car had me wondering how much he could bench press. I wondered how easy it would be for him to pick me up.

"Girl, you need to stop." I mumbled to myself as I took a sip of my hot tea.

He got in his car and sat there with the engine running for a moment. I couldn't actually see what he was doing so I imagined it involved his phone and a morning motivational playlist. A few more minutes passed by and I wondered if he had changed his mind. Then his taillights lit up and he pulled out of the driveway.

I sighed and sipped more of my tea.

6:45 pm Thursday

I sat down with my glass of wine just as he backed into the driveway. He sat in the car for a while. I imagined he was listening to a favorite song and didn't want to get out until it was over. When he got out, I saw that he was dressed for work. His dress shirt was rolled up at the sleeves, showing off his muscular forearms. His suit pants were the right kind of snug around his legs. When he bent into the back seat of his car, I got a lovely view of his ass in the black suiting fabric.

"Oh, that's nice."

He got his bags out and stood back up. He tossed his suit jacket over his shoulder. Then he shut the car door and locked the car. When he looked around, I leaned back from the window a bit. I didn't want him to see me watching him. He didn't look up. He just looked around again before walking to his side door.

7:45 am Friday

I was pondering breakfast and almost missed him. I heard his door shut and hustled over to my perch by the window. He was in a dark gray suit that looked to be tailored to his body. The jacket was buttoned and his tie was neatly tucked in. I couldn't help but laugh that he was brushing his hair as he walked to his car. He had his briefcase in his other hand. I wondered if he was running late. I wondered how long it took him to get to his office.

He sat in the car for a few minutes again. Then he pulled off.

6:00 pm Friday

He backed into the driveway just as I was getting ready to get up and get a glass of wine. I, of course, sat my ass back in my chair. He sat in the car for only a minute or two before getting out. His jacket was off and his sleeves were rolled up again. He looked tired. I could see his eyes were low. He was moving slowly. Then he yawned and I knew he was going inside for a nap. I wondered if he would get out of those clothes and shower first or he would just fall on his bed or couch as soon as he got inside. I sighed as he stood up straight with his briefcase and suit jacket. He locked his car and slowly headed to his side door.

"Sweet dreams, handsome neighbor."

7:30 am Saturday

My internal alarm clock never cared what day of the week it was. I was up with my cup of tea and a book when I saw him coming out of his side door. He was dressed for the gym, basketball shorts, and a tank top. I really wanted to reach out and touch his muscles. Instead, I just tried not to fog up the window as I watched him get in his car.

"Sheesh, girl. You act like you haven't seen a fine ass man before."

I didn't move even after fussing with myself. Even after he pulled out of the driveway. I sat there, with my face closer to the window than necessary, remembering his muscles and his mahogany skin. Finally, I sighed and leaned back in my chair. I wasn't hopeful about being able to refocus on the book I was reading.

1:15 pm Saturday

I missed him coming home but caught a glimpse of him when I was in my bedroom. He was doing yard work in his backyard. Part of me wanted to lean out of the other window so that I could get a better view.

"So, you can really be the crazy neighbor."

I sighed and shook my head. Instead, I leaned against the wall and watched him from the smaller side window. All he was doing was cutting the grass. I was still fascinated. It was hot and the sun was high without a cloud in sight. His shirt looked drenched in sweat. I watched patiently as he mowed. When he took a break, he drank some water and took his shirt off.

I swooned. "Good lord."

His chest was glorious. The smooth mahogany muscles were on full display. His back made my mouth water when he went back to mowing. The definition in his muscles was beautiful. He didn't look like a bodybuilder but his body definitely looked built. Not to the level that it was a turnoff. He was really just right.

I reached out and touched the window, wishing that I could touch him.

"Lawd, woman. I might need wine a little early today."

I didn't move towards the wine. Instead, I stayed there and watched him finish the lawn and then put his mower back in his shed. He did a quick lap around the lawn with the weed whacker before putting it away and going back into the house.

7:50 pm Saturday

The sound of laughter woke me up from a nap I hadn't planned on taking. I went to the side window and saw that he had several people over. They were all sitting around in chairs in his backyard.

I walked over to my open back window so I could hear better.

"Eli, where are you hiding that good Cognac?"

"If I told you, it wouldn't be hidden anymore."

"Man, what kind of host are you?"

"The kind that has plenty of liquor out for you to enjoy." He laughed.

His voice was deep and smooth, like velvet. His laugh made my clit throb. I sat down on the floor next to the window. After about ten minutes of listening to others talk, I got up and went to the side window. I could see him, dressed in a burgundy polo shirt and tan cargo shorts, sitting in a chair listening to whoever was talking. I wanted to go and sit in his lap. I hoped none of the women in the backyard had any claim to him.

"You'll probably never know because you'll never get up the nerve to approach him."

I pouted at my words. They were the truth though. I sighed and decided that I couldn't stand and watch him and his friends all night. Instead, I decided to take a shower. I decided to take a toy with me to work off some frustration.

9:35 pm Sunday

I sat the two trash bags I had in my hands down and took a breath. I saw that my downstairs neighbor had already taken the trash can to the curb. I sighed and prepared to pick the bags up again.

"Need some help?"

"Um…" I looked up and saw him walking down his driveway with his trash can.

"They look heavy."

His voice was melting my panties.

"They kinda are." I smiled.

He got close to me and grabbed one of the bags. He smiled and grabbed the other with the same hand.

"Thank you."

He smiled at me. "No problem."

He smelled like he had just gotten out of the shower. I tried not to be a weirdo and breathe him in too much as he walked past me. I watched him walk down to the curb. He tossed one of my bags in the can and then put the other bag on top. He left his can at the edge of his driveway and walked back up.

"I'm Elijah."

"Melinda."

"Nice to meet you." He looked at his hands. "I'd shake your hand but they are dirty from the trash."

I smiled. "It's okay."

"It was nice meeting you."

"Nice meeting you as well." I paused. "Thanks again for the help."

"You're welcome."

I watched Elijah walk back up his driveway for a few moments before forcing myself to not be a creep and go in the house.

7:30 pm Wednesday

Elijah pulled up in the driveway and I guessed that he had gone to the gym after work. When he got out and was wearing shorts and a tank top, I raised my glass.

"Ten points for me."

I sipped my wine and adjusted my chair so I could lean back and still see him getting his things out of his car. It had been two weeks since I bumped into him in the driveway. I kept up a regular routine of watching him come and go. I also made sure to dump my trash earlier so that I wouldn't bump into him again. He smelled too good and I was afraid I was going to try and bite him.

"He shouldn't look so delicious."

I took another sip of my wine as he locked his car and headed into the house.

4:30 pm Saturday

"Melinda."

I looked up from my phone when I heard Elijah's voice. He was walking across the parking lot to the front of the store. I smiled when he got closer to me. "Hi."

"Hi." He smiled. "How are you?"

"Good. How are you?"

"Pretty good. Running in here real quick." He looked around. "Headed to your car."

I shook my head. "I don't drive. I was calling a ride."

"If you are willing to wait a few minutes I can give you a ride. I'm only getting a few things."

My heart stopped at the thought of being in a car with him. "Sure. Thanks."

"I'll only be a few minutes." Elijah headed into the store.

I sat on the bench in front of the store and backed out of the rideshare app. I sent my best friend a quick text letting her know that I was getting a ride from my sexy neighbor. She responded quickly by reminding me not to bite him. I told her I would try to behave.

"Okay. I'm parked right over there."

I looked up and Elijah was standing in front of me. "That was quick."

"I only needed three things."

I stood up. Elijah pushed my cart as I walked with him over to his car. He loaded my bags into the trunk of his car and then let me in the passenger side. The inside of his car was as nice as I imagined. He kept it very clean. When he got in the car I wished I knew more about fragrances so that I could label what he smelled like. Whatever it was gently filled the car and was lovely.

He started the car and quickly turned down the music. "Sorry about that."

"It's okay." I smiled and watched him change the music on his phone before putting the phone down in the center console.

"I guess you not driving is why I only ever see one car at the house."

"Yeah. That's the lady downstairs." I glanced at him and then out the window. "I used to drive but when my last car died, I never got around to replacing it. I work from home so it hasn't been a big deal."

"What do you do?"

"Virtual Personal Assistant."

"Okay."

"What about you?"

"Account Executive."

"Interesting."

"You like working from home?"

"The dress code is lovely."

Elijah laughed. "Work in your pajamas a lot?"

"Yup." I smiled as I watched him turn down the street that led to our neighborhood. "My clients keep me busy but not too busy. I get to spend a lot of time reading and watching movies."

"You're a movie buff?"

"Yes."

Elijah pulled up to his driveway and backed in.

"I really appreciate the lift."

"Not a problem. Not like we weren't going to almost the same place."

I laughed. "True."

Elijah turned the car off. "I can help you with your bags."

"I can probably do it in one trip."

"But since you have help it'll definitely only take one trip."

I smiled. "That makes sense."

We got out of the car and Elijah helped me get my bags out of his trunk. It was a lot easier to make it up the steps since I wasn't loaded down with a ton of bags. Elijah carried most of them. He sat them down on the landing at the top of the steps.

I smiled at him. "Thank you."

"You're welcome." He smiled and nodded. "Have a good evening."

"You too."

I watched Elijah head down the steps and out of the house. I wished I had come up with a reason to talk to him for longer. I sighed and opened my door to take my groceries inside.

6:30 am Monday

I just happened to lean back to grab my tea off the table and luckily I was slowly moving back to the window because Elijah looked up at my window when he came out of the house. He kept looking while he walked to his car. I wasn't sure if he could see me or not. It didn't seem like he could. He didn't wave or anything. He was dressed for the gym. He stopped looking long enough to put his things in the back of his car. Then he looked up again for a few seconds before getting in his car. As usual, he sat there for a few minutes before finally pulling off.

"I wonder if he saw me or thinks I was watching."

I sighed and sat back in my chair.

8:30 pm Thursday

My doorbell rang and it almost scared the piss out of me. I wasn't expecting anyone. I hadn't ordered any food. I was thoroughly confused. The only reason I went down to answer it was because I knew that both my downstairs neighbor and Elijah were both home and hoped that one of them would hear me if I screamed.

Elijah smiled at me when I glanced through the curtain on the door at the bottom of the steps. I opened the door and smiled back at him.

"Hi."

"Hi. I hope I wasn't disturbing you."

"No. I was just reading."

"Oh. Okay."

We were quiet for a moment before I spoke up. "So, what's up?"

"I wanted to see if you would like to go to a movie with me."

"A movie?"

"Yeah. We could also grab a bite to eat too."

I smiled. "That sounds fun."

"Is tomorrow night too soon?"

"No. Tomorrow night is good for me."

"Great. It would be a late movie or late dinner."

"Either works for me."

"Okay. Great." Elijah smiled again. "I can come over and get you at seven."

"Okay. I'll be ready at seven."

"Great." He took a step back. "See you tomorrow at seven then."

"Okay. See you then."

I watched him turn and walk off the porch before I shut the door. I squealed as silently as I could. Then I took a few deep breaths before running up the steps to go and text my best friend.

6:10 pm Friday

I was like a junkie. I knew I was going to be seeing him for our date but I still had to sit in my seat and watch him when he pulled up in his driveway after work. Elijah sat in the car for almost five minutes before he got out this time. As he had begun to do, he looked up at my window and I instantly moved back a bit because I wasn't sure if he could see me or not. I was pretty sure he couldn't but I didn't want to take the chance. I giggled as he clapped his hands together and then turned to get his stuff out of the car. He moved faster than normal getting in the house. That prompted me to get up and finish getting myself together for our date.

10:15 pm Friday

After the movie, we went to a restaurant and ended up ordering appetizers and dessert. We split a jumbo popcorn at the movie. We spent all of the time we ate appetizers talking about the movie. When dessert was delivered, Elijah looked up at me.

"So, what else do you like to do for fun?"

I took a bite of my cake so that I could take that moment to figure out my answer. "Movies and books mostly. I haven't been getting out much lately."

"What did you do when you did get out?"

I laughed. "I hate clubs. I used to go see live music though. I like museums and galleries. It has been a while."

"I spend most of my time at work or at the gym. Every now and again I hang out with friends."

"What did you used to do?"

Elijah chuckled. "Sporting events. Concerts. Movies."

"All sound fun."

"So maybe I can talk you into going out with me again."

I smiled. "We haven't even finished the first date and you're planning the next one."

"I like to plan ahead." He winked at me.

"I like that."

"So, our second date can be to the museum and the third one we can catch a show down at the Pier."

I laughed and hoped it hid my blush. "Both sound great."

"Good."

We talked about music while we finished dessert. Then Elijah paid and we headed home. Our conversation continued all the way to my front door. After exchanging numbers, Elijah kissed me softly on the lips. It took everything in me to let the kiss remain as it was. I really wanted so much more.

He backed away and smiled. "Goodnight. I'll text you tomorrow."

"Okay. Goodnight." I tried not to smile like an idiot but I was still reeling from his kiss. His lips were so soft. I felt like I could spend hours kissing them. When I got inside the house, I touched my lips while walking up the steps to my apartment.

2:30 pm Sunday

At the moment I couldn't think of anything worse than having a creepy rideshare driver. That was probably because I was stuck with one. He kept looking at me through the rearview mirror.

"Looks like you had fun. You headed home?"

I cursed under my breath about how much fun I had at brunch with friends. I was lit from sangria but sobering up thanks to the creep driving me to my house. I decided to not answer his question and look out the window. It wasn't a good time to not have my headphones. I pulled out my phone and scrolled through social media.

"You look good in that dress."

I glanced up as he turned his head back to face the road. We were about five minutes from my apartment. I decided to text Elijah and see if he was home. The driver really creeped me out.

Me: Are you home?

Elijah: Yeah. Sitting out back with friends.

Me: Oh. Okay.

Elijah: Why? What's up?

Me: I'm almost home and my rideshare driver is a creep.

Elijah: Gotcha.

Elijah: How close are you?

Me: Three Minutes.

Elijah: Okay

"Your boyfriend shouldn't let you out of his sight. Or do you not have one?"

I tried not to roll my eyes too hard because I wasn't sure if he was an angry creep or just a super creepy creep. It was hard to tell and anything could set the angry ones off. As we pulled up in front of the house, I couldn't help but smile. The driver turned to look at me and say something but stopped when Elijah walked up to the door next to me. The driver unlocked the door and Elijah opened it.

"Thank you." I said to Elijah as he helped me out of the car.

Elijah didn't look at the creepy driver when he shut the car door. He smiled at me. "Come on."

I let Elijah put his arm around me and lead me up to his front steps. When I looked up on his porch, I saw two of his friends standing there. They were watching the car as it finally pulled off. "You were busy."

"Come and join us. We were just out back drinking and talking."

"I've had enough to drink."

Elijah nodded. "We probably have too. These fools gotta sober up cause they aren't staying here."

The guys on the porch laughed. A woman came to the door. "Did y'all scare off whoever needed it?"

"Yes." One of the guys answered.

"Y'all this is Melinda." Elijah introduced me to his friends. "Melinda, these are my crazy ass friends. These two are Sean and Kevin. This is Carla. Torian and Charles are still out back."

"Hi. Nice to meet you all."

"Did you have a creep driver? I had one last month that almost made me not want to use the service anymore." Carla shook her head.

I smiled. "I gotta remember to rate him zero so I don't get him again."

I followed Carla into the house. Elijah had his hand on the small of my back and it felt good. Since my only plan was to go into my apartment and try to calm down from being creeped out, hanging out with him and his friends sounded like a much better plan.

6:30 pm Sunday

"Are you loading my dishwasher?"

"Yes." I looked up as Elijah walked into the kitchen. He just walked Sean out. I knew it was just the two of us and I had nervous energy. I really wanted him to kiss me. Actually, I wanted him to do more than kiss me but I wasn't sure if I was still under the influence of all the sangria I had devoured. I had two glasses when I first arrived when Elijah admitted to making it from scratch and Torian raved about it. It was really good so I helped them polish it off and then we spent the rest of the time sobering up over good conversation.

"You don't have to do that."

"I don't mind helping." I reached for the rest of the

glasses that were on the counter. Everyone brought all their dishes and trash inside before they left. It was nice to see that Elijah had thoughtful friends. They were all really nice and funny. It only took me a few moments to realize they were the same bunch who were there when I was looking down from my window a few weeks earlier.

Elijah began to rinse the other dishes and hand them to me. When we finished he and I shared the sink to rinse our hands. He handed me the dish towel. Then he dried his hands on his pants and I burst out laughing.

He smiled. "What?"

"You could have shared the towel with me."

"I know."

I shook my head. "Thank you for allowing me to crash your gathering."

"Thank you for staying. I hope you enjoyed yourself."

"I did."

Elijah reached over and touched my cheek gently. "I want to kiss you but after the creep earlier I don't want to push."

I smiled and took a step closer to him. "Your advances are welcome."

Elijah smiled and leaned in to kiss me. At first, our lips touched and it was as sweet as our first kiss. Then I parted my lips slightly and that was the invitation he needed to deepen the kiss. Elijah slipped his arms around my waist and pulled me close. I hung my arms over his shoulders and got lost in the kiss. We kissed for a while before Elijah pulled away. I thought about catching my breath but when I looked into his dark eyes I grabbed him by the shirt and pulled him back close to me. I could feel how hard he was.

"Mel..."

"Yes." I nodded before kissing him.

Elijah's hands were on my thighs within seconds of our lips touching. He picked me up and carried me upstairs to his bedroom. Our kiss stopped long enough for him to sit me down on the bed and take his shirt off. Then I pulled him down on top of me. We kissed and I unzipped my dress. Once I did that, Elijah took over getting me out of the dress. My bra and panties were next to go. He kissed his way up my thigh before putting his face between my legs. I moaned and began to rub the back of his head. Elijah used his tongue to tease me into a frenzy before focusing on my clit and brought me to orgasm.

"Delicious." Elijah kissed my thigh before standing up and taking off his pants and boxer briefs. He got a condom from his nightstand. Then he looked at me. "You good?"

I nodded and smiled.

"You ready?" Elijah hovered over me. He leaned his head down and took one of my nipples in his mouth. I moaned my affirmative response and spread my legs for him. He slowly eased his way inside me. As he did, he buried his face in my neck. "Shit girl. You feel so good."

I moaned as he pulled out a little and then eased back in. He did that a few more times before he picked up his pace. He grabbed my thigh and pulled my leg up over his arm. I rocked my hips to meet each of his strokes and moaned each time our bodies crashed together. It felt so good. I couldn't help but keep kissing his shoulder while his lips were all over my neck and chest. Each stroke pushed me closer and closer to the edge until I climaxed. I felt myself tighten around him as I cried out.

"Jesus, Mel. Fuck." Elijah thrust into me a few more times before he came. We lay next to each other for a few minutes, catching our breath.

Then I sat up. I pointed to a door. "Is that the bathroom?"

"Yup."

I got up and stumbled a little on my way to the door. I could hear Elijah chuckle. "Don't laugh at me."

"My bad."

I went to the bathroom and washed my hands. Elijah was coming over from the bed when I opened the door. I had to try hard not to swoon at how wonderful his body looked.

"Take a shower with me."

I smiled. "Um… okay."

"I'll try my best to behave myself."

I laughed. "It's okay if you struggle with that a bit."

"Just a bit." Elijah kissed me and led me back into the bathroom.

6:30 am Monday

It was nice watching Elijah get ready for his day while sitting on his bed. He didn't have a hard time talking me into spending the night. I enjoyed being wrapped around his body instead of the body pillow on my bed. I got dressed while he was in the bathroom.

"So, no playing hooky from work today?" Elijah looked at me as he came back into the bedroom.

"Nope." I smiled.

"You sure?" He slipped his arms around me and started to kiss me on my neck.

I giggled. "You gotta get to the gym. I need to get my day started."

"Okay. Okay." Elijah groaned. "I'll walk you home."

"I live next door."

"So. I'm a gentleman and I'm going to walk you home."

I sighed and waited while he grabbed his gym bag and garment bag. Then Elijah walked me next door. He stood at the porch steps while I opened the door. He was putting his stuff in the back of his car when I got up to my window. When he looked up I leaned close to the window so that he could see me. He smiled and I waved. Then he got in his car and, after a few moments, backed out of the driveway. I smiled and went to get ready for my day.

7:15 pm Friday

I watched Elijah pull up in the driveway. He sat in his car for a few minutes before finally turning it off and getting out. Instead of going to his house, he walked over to mine. I smiled and waited for the doorbell to ring before heading to the door. I went down the steps and opened the door.

"Hey." Elijah smiled at me.

"Hi."

"I know I said we should spend an evening apart."

"You did." I nodded thinking of the conversation we had before he went to work earlier that morning. We had spent every night together since Sunday. He took me out to dinner twice and we cooked together in his kitchen the other nights. I wasn't upset that he wanted a break. I was getting too comfortable myself. Even with the idea in my head that we wouldn't be together that evening, I still cooked enough food for the both of us.

"But all I want to do is sit and hear about your day."

I smiled and stepped to the side so he could come in. "Come up. I made dinner."

Elijah stepped inside. He shut the door behind him and followed me up the stairs. "You really made dinner?"

"I did. Barbecue chicken. I made enough for both of us." I pointed to the bathroom when we got inside my apartment. "You can wash your hands and come sit at the table."

"You sure you aren't going to get sick of me?"

I turned and smiled at him. "I'm not sure of anything but let's see what happens."

Elijah smiled. "Agreed."

The End

Other works by Turtleberry

Are You Okay?

Nobody's Somebody

Sweet Turtleberry Jam Volume One

These Women Book One

These Women Book Two

These Women Book Three

Happily Ever After

Sweet Turtleberry Jam Volume Two

Catching Evie

Needs To Be Met

Love Unexpected

Lena's Chance At Love

Both Sides Of Me

Whiskey Kisses

Halloween Spice

It For Me

Days of Summer

One More Kiss

The Friend

Finding Love

www.sweetturtleberry.com